Fiddlesticks!

For Margot – S.T.

To my Mum and Dad and Chrissy – S.G.

Written with my hat raised to the very funny British songwriters, Flanders and Swann.
The idea for this story came to me while listening to a song of theirs called THE GAS MAN COMETH. S.T.

SIMON AND SCHUSTER
First published in Great Britain in 2014 by Simon and Schuster UK Ltd
1st Floor, 222 Gray's Inn Road, London WC1X 8HB
A CBS Company
Text copyright © 2014 Sean Taylor
Illustrations copyright © 2014 Sally Anne Garland
The right of Sean Taylor and Sally Anne Garland to be identified as the author and illustrator of this work
has been asserted by them in accordance with the Copyright, Designs and Patents Act, 1988
All rights reserved, including the right of reproduction in whole or in part in any form
A CIP catalogue record for this book is available from the British Library upon request
ISBN 978-0-85707-614-4 (HB) 978-0-85707-615-1 (PB) 978-1-4711-1838-8 (eBook) · Printed in China · 10 9 8 7 6 5 4 3 2 1

Fiddlesticks!

Sean Taylor & Sally Anne Garland

SIMON AND SCHUSTER
London   New York   Sydney   Toronto   New Delhi

Mouse stepped outside his lovely little house.
Everything about it was just right.
And he felt glad about that.

Except . . .

He noticed one of the windows
was a little bit crooked.

He tried to pull it straight.
But he couldn't.
He was too small.

So he said,
"FIDDLESTICKS!"

And he was pleased to see Bear.
Bear was big and strong.

With a little push, he put
the window straight.

Except . . .

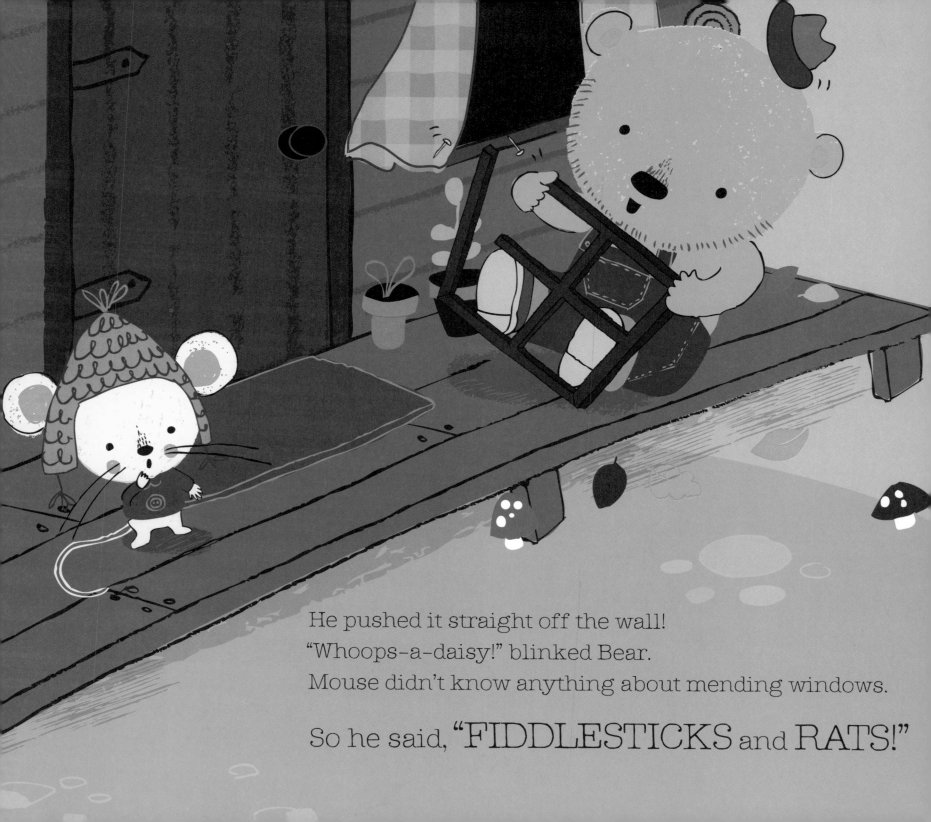

He pushed it straight off the wall!
"Whoops-a-daisy!" blinked Bear.
Mouse didn't know anything about mending windows.

So he said, "FIDDLESTICKS and RATS!"

And it was lucky
Squirrel came past.

Squirrel was good at climbing
and doing woodwork.

With a bit of hammering
and tip-tapping nails,
the window was ready
to go back up.

Except . . .

Squirrel tip-tapped one of the nails right through a water pipe!

"Deary, deary me!" sniffed Squirrel.

Mouse didn't know how to
stop water squirting out.

So he said, "FIDDLESTICKS,
RATS and HOPSCOTCH!"

And he was pleased when Otter showed up.
Otter was good at swimming. And he knew
all about fitting
and fixing pipes.

He climbed up, and just
about stopped the
water squirting.

Except....

He put dirty paw prints all up and down the walls.
"Oh. Sorry about that!" said Otter.

Cleaning the walls didn't look as
if it was going to be easy at all.

And Mouse said,

"FIDDLESTICKS, RATS, HOPSCOTCH and NANG DANG DARN IT!"

So it was a good thing that Moose looked in.

Moose was tall and good at painting and decorating. He whistled a tune and swished his brush.

And soon the walls looked as good as new.

Except . . . .

When he stood up,
his antlers went right
through the roof!
"Oh my gracious!" exclaimed Moose.

And Mouse didn't know what to say.

He was lost for words.

And he couldn't bear to look at his poor broken house a minute longer.

"I know they were trying to help," he said to himself,
"but those friends of mine have messed things up."

It wasn't until the sun was going down that Mouse decided
he'd better go home and try to sort things out.

And that was when he discovered that his friends didn't only mess things up.

"WOW KERPOW!"
cried Mouse.
"Thank you, everybody!
That's the best house ever!"

And it was.

Except . . .

In fact, they'd built him a really quite amazing new house.

When Mouse stepped inside, he noticed
the door was a little bit crooked.
So he said, "FIDDLESTICKS!" and he
wondered about asking Bear to put it right.

But then he thought again.
And he decided that a crooked door didn't –
actually – look too bad.